How Many Animals?

by Joe Margolin

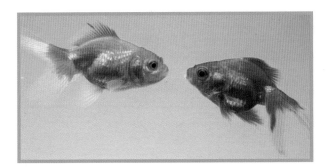

HOUGHTON MIFFLIN

BOSTON

My Words

puppies

one

two

three

four

five

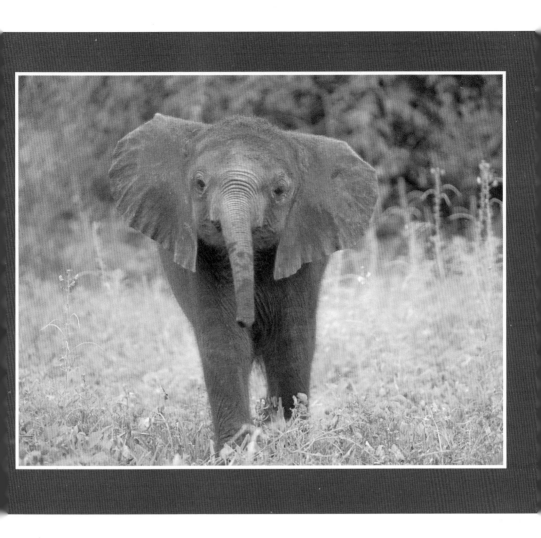

I see one elephant.

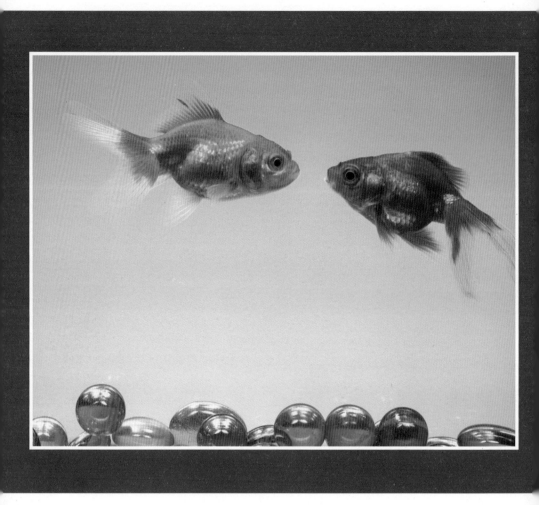

I see two fish.

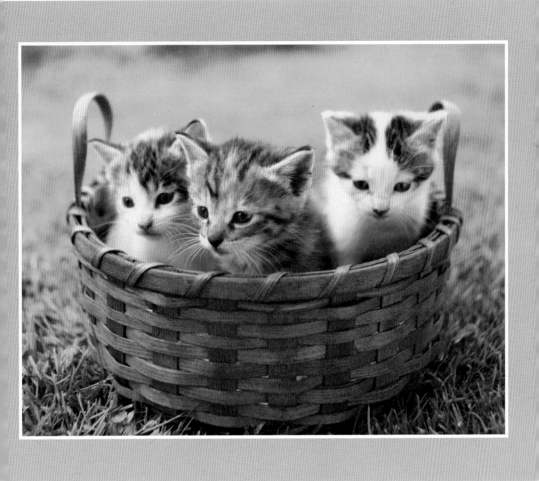

I see three cats.

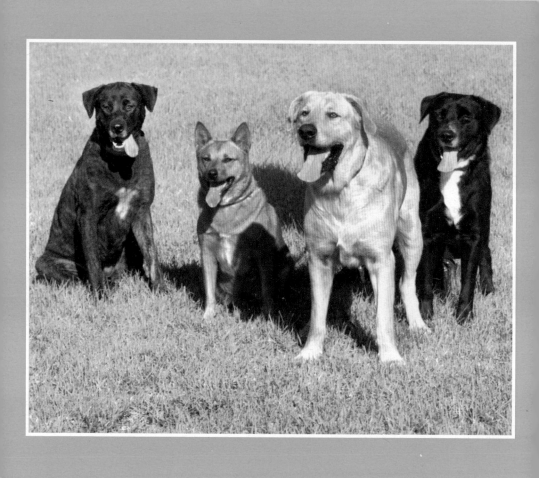

I see four dogs.

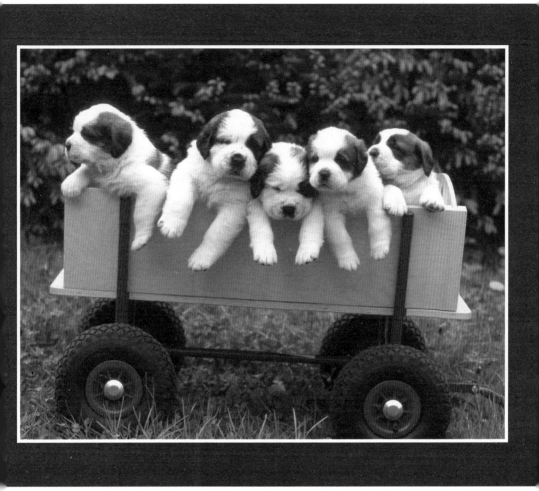

I see five puppies.

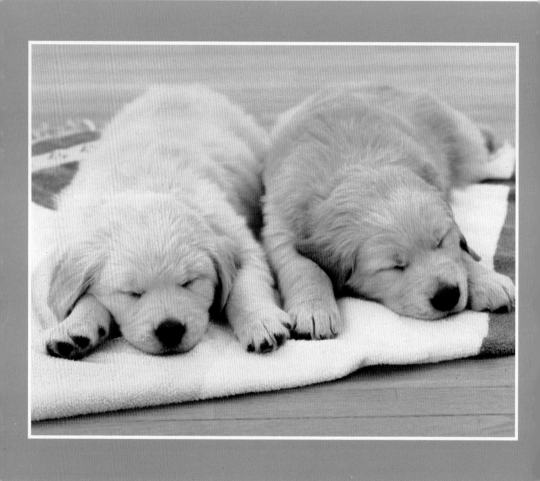

How many do you see?